Billionaire Daddy Series

CEO Billionaire Daddy
(Book 1)

S.E. Riley

The Redherring Publishing House

CEO Billionaire Daddy
(Book 1)

Table of Contents

Prologue

Lillian stepped into the Poet's Brew coffeehouse and inhaled the heady aroma of brewing coffee and buttered scones. It had been too long since she'd come in here. When had she last been in here? Probably a year ago, when she was with her older brother Tyler for the Christmas holidays. He'd made her feel like his kid sister all over again despite all the growing up she'd done, and while she loved him dearly, she was glad he wasn't here to make her feel that way today. He was only seven years older, but he made a big deal of it, and she wanted time to celebrate this milestone as an adult. Tyler forgot she wasn't the little kid he'd raised alone after their parents died in a car accident. Being here alone for once made her feel more like the adult she was, and it seemed like the perfect way to celebrate her return home.

She stepped up to the counter and placed her order, heading over to the pickup counter with her gaze fixed on her phone screen. Job hunting had proven difficult, and she hoped the employer she'd interviewed with last week would call back with a job offer. As she scrolled through emails, she ran into a solid, warm shape.

Gasping, she looked up to see who she'd run into, an apology on her lips. The apology died when she saw familiar gray eyes and dark, neatly combed hair that always seemed to curl at the ends. She shivered, remembering how those gray eyes had fixed on her the summer she'd had a gap year to save for college. He hadn't been able to stop looking at her when they'd gone to the pool or taken runs together.

Tyler had griped about it teasingly, and she'd daydreamed that those looks meant more than they probably had. She doubted the man who'd been like a second older brother when she was a kid had developed a similar crush on her as she'd had on him during high school. Still did, if her inability to think of something to say was anything to go on.

She finally managed to stop gaping like an idiot and squeaked, "Atticus?"

He frowned down at her. "Lillian? When did you get home?"

"Two days ago. I've been busy job hunting," she admitted. "I should've thought to call and let you know I'd come back."

"That would've been nice." His gaze raked over her. "But it's not as if you're still a little kid texting your brother or your brother's best friend to tell them you made it to the theater safely when you were a senior."

She flushed and stared down at the ground. "I hated it when you two made me do that."

He laughed. "I know, but we wanted to know you were safe."

True, she understood why he and Tyler were overly protective of her, but she hadn't wanted Atticus to see her as a little kid he needed to watch out for. She still didn't, but running into him probably didn't help solidify her image as an independent woman he no longer needed to baby.

"Do you have a minute?" Atticus's low voice snapped her out of her thoughts.

She looked up at him with a smile and tucked an unruly auburn curl out of her face. "Yeah. Do you?"

"I can make one. Perks of being the CEO of a successful company."

"And yet you're still in here getting your usual." She eyed his cup. "Hold on. I need to get my order."

He walked her to the counter. "It really is good to see you,

Lil. I see you haven't changed your habits one bit. Still glued to walking while staring at a screen or a book."

The tips of her ears heated. She looked away and went to collect her order when they called her name. Behind her, she thought she heard Atticus mutter something about making a rule against walking and reading at the same time if she were his, but she shook off the idea.

He wouldn't say something like that.

Atticus saw her as the little sister he'd never had. Being ten years older, he probably wouldn't see her as a twenty-three-year-old woman with an interest in finding the right man to settle down with. He could have anyone, anyway. He wouldn't want the girl he'd grown up with and saw as a kid's sister.

"So, what are you doing these days? You mentioned job hunting. Didn't you finish your degree in interior design?" Atticus took her elbow and steered her toward a table.

She let him pull her chair out and push her in once she was seated. "I did, but I'm not having any luck with jobs."

"Any examples you can show me?"

"Promise not to laugh." She set her phone on the table.

He eyed her. "Why would I laugh, Lillian? I'm sure you've worked hard on your work, just as you always have. Let me see."

She opened the folder with photos from some of the redecorating and design work she'd done in school and handed him the phone. Sipping at her coffee while he looked, she tried not to squirm in the seat. A flush warmed her ears and then her cheeks as he looked through everything in silence. Finally, he pushed the phone back across the table and took a sip of his own coffee, his gaze fixed on her.

"It's not very good, I know," she whispered. "That might be why I'm not—"

"They're very good, Lil. Top notch work, actually. Your inability to find a job has nothing to do with your talent." He continued to watch her for a moment, those gray eyes searching. Lillian squirmed some more in her seat. Then he

3

pulled a business card from his pocket and handed it to her. "Use the email on the card. Send me your resume and portfolio."

She frowned. "Why?"

"Because my head of design needs an assistant, and I think you'd be perfect."

Lillian steeled for a moment. "This seems like a huge coincidence...I don't know."

"Sometimes coincidences happen. I wasn't expecting to run into you or hear that you're still looking for work, but this right here..." he tapped on his business card that was in front of her, "...seems like a good solution to both of our problems."

She didn't want handouts. Besides, a position as assistant to a director? She was fresh out of school and couldn't possibly be qualified. Furthermore, there was the little problem of a clash between her career and the desire for him that obviously hadn't faded. Seeing him again forced her to admit he'd only grown more attractive to her over time. This would be a disaster.

"Atticus, come on...I—"

He raised a brow. "I wasn't asking, Lillian. You need a job. My design director needs an assistant. She'll like you. Apply. I'm not handing you anything. You'll have to interview her and impress her yourself. I don't make a habit of handing things out to anyone, especially not without proof it's merited."

That much was true. Atticus never handed anything to anyone, just as no one had ever handed anything to him. It's what he'd always liked about her brother—the two of them knew what it was to claw their way to the top and to fight tooth and nail to survive.

Atticus had been better at it, but the two had held their own together through the years. If he was telling her to apply, not just politely suggesting it, then he wanted her there because he thought she could do the job.

The heat in her cheeks traveled down her neck. She must look like a cherry tomato by now. That only worsened the situation. He thought too highly of her. She wasn't the right one for this.

"Is there a reason you don't think you'd be a fit for the job?" he murmured.

She squirmed in the seat. Why did he always have to be so perceptive when it came to her? "Well…"

"Besides an abominable lack of self-confidence, Lillian."

She couldn't tell him she was worried she'd never be able to focus if she had to work with him, and she *did* need the job desperately. If he would not hand her anything and she'd either stand or fall on her own merit, she could be professional for the sake of her career, and mounting bills and debt.

"No," she admitted quietly. "I guess there's not."

He stood with a broad smile. "Good. I can't guarantee you the job. That's not how my company runs. If you're the best candidate, though, I can promise you'll get it. I expect the resume and digital copies of your portfolio in my inbox by the end of the evening, little miss. Got it?"

She ducked her head, hating the sound of that childhood nickname on his lips; *little miss*. That confirmed it. He still thought of her as a kid sister, not as a woman he might see himself dating.

She needed to get over this silly infatuation with him. He'd never see her the way she wanted him to, and she was setting herself up for heartbreak if she didn't stop hoping for it.

"Got it."

"Good." He walked away.

She sat there a moment longer, wishing she could get Atticus off her mind and out of her imagination.

He wasn't meant for her.

Tyler would have a fit if anything ever happened, and Atticus would never risk Tyler's wrath, even if he saw her as more than a little girl now.

Any chance with him was doomed already. Sighing, she

finished her coffee and left the shop. She'd turn in her resume tonight. Even if she could never have him, she could still have the job he'd offered if she tried.

Chapter 1

Two years later

Lillian stood on the pier waiting for him when Atticus disembarked from his private charter ship. He descended the gangplank, watching as she stared at him for a long moment before shaking her head and stepping forward with a smile to greet him.

He spoke first, beating her to a greeting. "Lil. How do you like my island?"

"It's…" She laughed. "I guess I should've known it would be spectacular. Every other location you've built has been, and you did, build a private getaway on the other side of the island. But I have to admit I was a bit shocked when I saw it."

"Wait until you see the main island. Those resorts and hotels were built before you started with us, and they won't be as modern as this one, but I think you'll like them."

"I didn't realize we were planning a trip over there."

"I was." He smiled down at her. "I thought it would be nice to go together, just us."

She looked away, flushing. "Oh...I...is there time?"

"We'll make time. I want to show them off a bit, especially since you'll be taking over Marie's position as design director next year."

Her shoulders relaxed. "Oh, I see." Lillian looked around before changing the subject. "Was it a good trip, boss?"

"Atticus," he corrected mildly. "This counts as off work, Lillian."

She lifted one shoulder in a half shrug and ducked her head, the setting sun glinting off her red-gold hair as she returned to her earlier discomfort.

He frowned at her dismissal. After two years of working together, she still seemed uneasy with him outside of the formalities of the office. They worked together wonderfully, and in a few more years, when his head designer retired, she would take over that role. He loved how easy it was to work with her, but he hated how tense she became when he tried to make things more personal.

"A verbal response, not a shrug, Lil."

He still remembered the first day he'd seen her again after two years of studying abroad. She'd no longer been the little girl he remembered from childhood. She'd been much more outgoing with him back then. Sweet, innocent, and talkative. Now she was reserved, and anxious outside of work. He disliked the change and often wondered what had caused it, but he couldn't seem to tease it out of her, so he'd backed off.

She stared at the ground and shifted, but didn't answer.

"Very well. Are we pushing buttons today?" He almost wished the answer was yes, because at least then she'd be acting more like the girl he'd known since they were younger.

"No button pushing today, I promise." She smiled shyly, her green eyes flicking up to his and then away. "I'm on the clock, remember? You made me promise not to clock out before I drove over to pick you up."

He suppressed a groan. He'd only told her to convince her to come in place of his chauffeur. The drive back to the hotel was long, and he'd wanted to get her alone before they really dove into the project. His reasons for being here went beyond overseeing the final touches on designs and the first month of operation. This time, he would use this trip to perform a miracle.

He was done waiting for Lillian to realize that he was interested and trying to subtly hint it to her, too. He'd be cautious in his approach and ease her into the idea, but he was almost certain that the young woman currently unlocking her little sedan was also interested and just didn't want to admit it. She needed coaxing, but she was interested. He'd caught her sneaking glances when she thought he wasn't looking.

Lillian Miller liked him but had convinced herself she couldn't have him, just like she always convinced herself she couldn't afford to eat that last piece of cake on her birthday. He needed to deal with that misconception soon. "I made you promise because I wanted to compensate you for the drive out. I did not tell you that because I wanted to spend the drive home in business mode."

She opened her car door but paused, that lovely flush back in her cheeks. "You didn't?"

"No, I did not." He held out a hand for the keys.

She backed away a bit to look up at him. "You're paying me to drive."

"Not anymore. You're off the clock now, little miss." He crooked a finger. "Keys, please."

She bit her lip and glanced at the car, as if uncertain what to do. He waited quietly, trying not to think about how much he wanted to pull her lip from between her teeth and kiss her senseless.

Finally, Lillian dropped the keys into his outstretched hand, a tiny shiver working through her slight frame. "Yes, sir."

"Do we need to have another chat about not behaving like an employee when it's just us? We're friends too, Lil, not just employer and employee."

The blush deepened, nearly hiding her freckles. "Why did you want me to drive over if you didn't plan on resting?"

"Because I wanted time to talk to you on the trip. You know I dislike chauffeurs." He rounded the car and opened the passenger's door for her. "Hop in, please."

She brushed past him with another tiny shiver and climbed into the car. He reached across to buckle her in, catching the tiny hitch in her breathing when he did so with a tiny smile.

He shouldn't tease her about it, but he couldn't resist.

"Something the matter?"

"No, s—"

He raised a brow.

"No," she murmured. "Can we go back to the hotel now?"

"Better idea. We'll go back to my mansion on the other side of the island. I was going to invite the staff to stay there in the extra rooms until the hotel is finished, anyway." He pulled away from the docks and headed inland.

Lillian toyed with her skirt's hem. She often did that when she was alone with him, and he wasn't sure if she was nervous or simply needed something to occupy her hands. Reaching over, he laid a hand over hers, guessing that it was nerves, not the need to occupy herself.

"You seem nervous. What's wrong?"

"I'm just..." She sighed and shivered. "I'm fine. Just nervous about the project. Like always...The last few weeks before a grand opening are always stressful."

"I see. Perhaps we can ease the stress. Did you pack a swimsuit?"

A furrow appeared between her brows. "I...why?"

"I thought we could relax in the pool at my place."

"Oh." She stared out the window. "If you like."

"It's not always about what I like, Lil. Do you want to?"

She pursed her lips. "You're sure it would be okay?"

"More than okay."

"Then yes, I would." A tiny smile softened the corners of her mouth.

He gave her some space, briefly letting the silence stretch between them. Then he confronted the strange tension that had been building between them over the last two years. He'd promised himself he was done waiting and meant it.

"You're nervous around me when we're not in a work setting."

"What?" Her head jerked up. "No, I—"

He frowned at her. "Lillian Miller, the next words out of your mouth had best not be a lie or an excuse."

"I...Well, what if I am?"

"I don't like that very much, and I hate to think I might be the reason. Am I?"

"Not exactly." Her voice barely rose above a whisper. "You've been a great boss..."

"Only a great boss?"

"And a good friend."

"No one would know that, looking at how you act around me outside of work. What is it that puts you on pins and needles with me as soon as I'm not playing the role of your boss?"

"I just..." She pulled her knees to her chest. "I don't know, Atticus. I feel like you see me as that little kid that tagged along with you and Tyler, and I don't know how to act with you in private now that I'm...well, I'm not a kid. You still call me little miss, like you did when we were kids, so obviously—" She cut herself off with a sigh.

He glanced over to find her attention fixed on the road ahead instead of him. "I do not see you as a child, Lil. You became a lovely young woman in the time you were away, something I am very much aware of. I call you that because it's always been an endearment between us, an endearment that has more to do with your height than your age. I didn't know it upset you."

She blushed and turned her face away from him. "It...well, if you put it that way, I guess it doesn't."

He pulled into the driveway of his mansion and stopped the car, turning to face her. "I want this awkwardness to end, Lil. I don't like it and intend to remove every reason for it. Is thinking I see you as a child the only issue?"

She wouldn't look at him.

"You don't have to tell me now. That's your choice, but think very carefully before you try to lie to me again," he warned. "You know I don't tolerate lies to avoid difficult truths."

"I can't...I can't talk about this." Her voice shook, and she

11

reached for the door handle.

"I'll come around to open it for you. We'll table this for now, but Lil?"

She finally turned her gaze back to his.

"It's not being tabled forever, understand?"

She nodded, looking anywhere but him.

He ignored the lack of verbal response just this once. He climbed out and went around to open her door.

Then he retrieved her suitcase and guided her inside. He'd dig into her anxious response to him more deeply later. He'd clearly failed to make his interest apparent, but he'd rectify that situation quickly so that there could be no doubt in her mind that he saw her as a woman—a woman he respected and wanted. For now, he just wanted to get her to bed, so she'd be well-rested for what lay ahead.

Chapter 2

A week after their arrival on the island, Atticus knocked on the doorframe of the main office of his new resort and hotel. Lillian sat at a desk bent over design plans. This was the first project for one of his chains of resorts and hotels that she'd taken the lead on for her direct supervisor, Marie, and he'd never seen her so tightly wound. Her shoulders were hunched, and she was going through the swatches of paint colors and carpeting options. She'd been reviewing them last night too.

At his knock, she jumped, her gaze flying to his. "Boss!" She put a hand to her heart. "I hadn't seen you there."

He stepped inside and closed the door. "You went over those same swatches last night. Is something wrong?"

"No, no. Just making certain these are our best options before I present them to you. We need to send them off to the team for final purchases. The paint crew's coming in three days, and they need to mix the paint batches before they come over here."

"I approved the colors last week and sent them off to the team already." He strode over to the desk and bent over to look, brushing her arm with his casually. "You're worrying too much."

She twisted to stare up at him. "You did what? But sir, those were preliminary options. I just wanted you to let me know what you thought. I hadn't decided for certain that they were our best—"

He laid a finger on her lips with a slight smile. "Shhh. First of all, we're in private, Lillian. We don't need titles. Second, they were the best. This isn't the first chain hotel or resort I've opened, nor is it the first luxury resort. I know what I'm doing. Besides, you showed me all the options months ago and sent me the one you thought might be the best choice. I agreed and sent it off. Then I told you I thought it was a solid choice."

"But solid doesn't mean the best," she whispered against his finger.

"It does when I say it." He picked up the swatches and dumped them into the garbage can beside the desk. "I have already decided, little miss. Stop worrying. The crews will be here with all the essential supplies over the next week or two. Let's focus on supervising and planning for the grand opening."

She stared at the garbage can for a long moment, a protest clear in the tight press of her full lips.

He reached out and took her chin, turning her face and her gaze back to him. "Eyes on me, not the trash can. Everything in there is no longer of importance. It's been handled. Now, what do you have for the grand opening?"

Her stare seemed a little unfocused, as if she was shocked by his boldness today. Well, little surprise. He'd abandoned his usual subtlety to be very clear with her as part of his new goal to have her as his by the end of this trip. She was probably still a bit confused since he hadn't yet declared that intent. He wasn't yet certain of the right moment to do it and was hoping to ease her into it with clearer hints to give her time to refuse if he'd read her wrong. So far, she hadn't protested his overtures, though she'd protested plenty about the design and showed more of that shy side he'd only ever seen when she was with him.

Atticus would tell her soon. There was little doubt in his mind now that he'd read the situation correctly.

"Lillian," he pressed.

"What?"

"The grand opening."

She flushed and tried to pull away. He didn't let her.

"Atticus," she whispered. "What are you doing?"

He grinned. "Asking you to share your thoughts on arranging the grand opening. We only have two months to put it together while the decorating crew are finalizing on things."

Her blush deepened, and she dropped her gaze to his Rolex. "That doesn't...you don't need to...I mean, this isn't very professional."

He put her out of her misery and released her, watching her shoulders slump in relief. He didn't leave her to revert to her usual professional self, and he pulled his chair around the desk to sit closer to her than was technically necessary. If she didn't like it, she could say so and put an end to his flirtations. Otherwise, he didn't plan to give her time to retreat into her shell of propriety to escape his intentions or her feelings about them. "Show me what you've worked out."

She fiddled with the portfolio's pages, her hair falling in a sheet to hide her face from him. The unruly curls never stayed put, even when she put it up. Today, her hair was loose in its usual wild self. He reached out to tuck it back behind her ear with a smile. He'd always liked that hair of hers. It was easily one of her best features.

Her fair skin flushed again, momentarily washing out the freckles. "It's fine in my face. I don't mind, really."

"I know that. The plans?"

She slid the portfolio over. "I thought we could open the casino attached to the hotel to the clients. Serve champagne and hoers d'oeuvres before dinner and end the evening with a nice catered dinner."

"That sounds like a good plan." He leaned closer until he could smell the rose perfume she liked to wear. "What else? Any specific plans for the meal or before dinner refreshments?"

"Since the clients will be wealthy, we should plan to dazzle." She settled a little, though she still cast him uneasy glances when it became clear he wasn't interested in leaving the usual space between them as they worked. "Armand de Brignac for the champagne before dinner and a glass of sparkling wine for those who would prefer it. I thought we could serve caviar *crème fraîche* tartlets and figs with bacon and chile for the *hoers d'oeuvres*. It gives two options in case anyone's averse to caviar."

"All excellent choices."

She glanced over at him. "May I ask why you wanted me to plan this instead of your marketing team or personal assistant? I know Marie often helps pitch in, but...I'm not Marie, and I don't do this stuff much."

"You've watched Marie do it, and since I plan to give you her position in a year when she retires, you should learn. You're doing a wonderful job. We'll let the team handle sorting out who will cater and all the finer details. I just want you to help design the party, the decor, the flow of the meal, that sort of thing."

She bit her lower lip. "I don't know if I can—"

"You don't have to. All that matters is that I'm confident you can and have you on the job." He leaned closer, frowning. "I don't want to overload you, but I know you can handle it, Lil. You're good at this, and you've already put together exactly what I'd hoped you would."

Her gaze dropped to the desk, and her head dipped, sending her hair into her face again. "Really?"

He brushed it behind her ear once more with a fond smile. This woman really was something else. She had an air of innocence and humility about her that was attractive, but it left a twinge of frustration deep inside every time she talked down about herself. Once she was his, he would make sure that stopped. "Really. Do you think I'd lie to you?"

She lifted one shoulder. "As my boss or as my..."

He raised a brow.

The adorable flush was back. "N-no."

"Good. Then accept the compliment because you've earned it."

"Yes, sir." She shuffled through the papers.

He watched her in silence for a long moment. The way her mouth tightened in uncertainty left him wanting to kiss away the stress that left her so concerned she'd mess this up. If he didn't know she needed a bit of time to become accustomed to how he'd changed his behavior, he'd do it too. "Good girl. Let's take a look at the rest of these plans, then, shall we?"

She peeked up at him through her lashes. "Atticus?"

He smiled encouragingly, pleased that she'd called him by his name instead of using more formal addresses for him. "Yes?"

"You're...something's different today, isn't it?"

"Yes."

"It was yesterday too."

"Yes."

"What's changed?" Her teeth worried at her lower lip.

He reached out and gently pulled her lip free from her teeth with the pad of his thumb before she could cause any damage. "Don't you know?"

A hint of a blush tinged her cheeks as she nodded no.

"I see." He leaned back, giving her a little space. "You know. You just want to hear me say it."

She ducked her head, shifting in her seat. "No, never mind. It was a silly question."

"No, it wasn't." He tipped her chin back up. "Why don't you want to vocalize what's changed, Lillian?"

She swallowed hard. "I...we're at work, Atticus."

"So if we were in my home or my apartment back in New York, you'd ask what you really want to know?" He narrowed his eyes. "No lies, Lillian, remember? That's the first rule of engagement with me."

She chewed on the inside of her cheek and then sighed. "I don't need to know," she finally muttered. "Let's just focus on work."

He laughed. "I think you're just afraid of the answer and what that answer might mean."

17

He didn't say anything more, just grinned. He'd let it go, for now. He turned his attention back to the high-level planning for the grand opening. Time enough to whittle away at her objections and defenses over the next couple of weeks they'd be here. He didn't have to rush, though he could admit a large part of him wanted her as his as soon as possible.

Chapter 3

Lillian sat at her desk in the manager's office, laptop open, but she wasn't thinking about anything on the screen. Instead, she was contemplating Atticus's behavior in the last week. She couldn't lie to herself or Atticus, even if she could refuse to give Atticus answers to his probing questions of late. She couldn't avoid the answers in her own mind, though. His behavior had been decidedly aimed at getting her attention.

Since their conversation in the car on the trip up here from the docks and their first meeting in this office, he'd taken every opportunity he could to touch her, though he remained professional in front of the rest of the staff. In private was another matter. She blushed, thinking of his teasing and featherlight touches in contrast to his firm tone of command and demand for her attention. There was no question of whether he had her focus. He definitely did.

There were a thousand reasons she shouldn't—no, couldn't—give in. Even though it had been a fantasy of hers to have him notice her this way, she couldn't actually reach out and grasp at it now that it was in front of her. He was like a brother.

Tyler, her real flesh-and-blood brother, would probably kill her and Atticus too if he ever caught wind of anything between them. She didn't want to disappoint or anger Tyler. Not after he'd paid half her way through college and done everything in his power to take care of her after their parents' deaths, it had been hard for him, and he'd made many sacrifices.

It was the main reason he wasn't rich like Atticus.

Taking care of her had knocked him back a few years in his law career, and even now, looking out for her had prevented him from climbing the corporate ladder at his law firm as quickly as he might have wanted to. Worse still, Atticus was her boss. It wouldn't be professional.

She knew all the reasons she shouldn't, but the truth was that all the reasons paled when he touched her or spoke to her in that low, commanding timbre. She didn't want to move away or say no, which was the problem. She shifted in her seat with a sigh. He had to remain the subject of her fantasies and dreams, not the subject of real life romantic attachment.

A knock at the door startled her out of her reverie. She looked up to find the object of her musings standing in the door in a crisply ironed dress shirt, an expensive suit, and his usual Rolex. His gray eyes remained firmly on her, and his lips curled into a slight smile of greeting. What would it be like to kiss that full mouth of his? Would he be a gentle kisser or demanding and passionate as he was in his work? The thoughts were as intrusive as the blush that rose unbidden to her cheeks as she stared at the man she'd been fantasizing about for more than a decade. These thoughts had no place in her job. She needed to get a grip, but for the life of her, she couldn't stop staring. She opened her mouth to say something and then closed it.

He raised a brow and walked into the small office. "Something to say, Lillian? You look a little flushed."

She stared down at her lap, the heat in her cheeks intensifying. "I...good morning, boss."

"Good morning, Atticus," he corrected. "But good morning to you, too, little miss. I came to see if you were ready for the tour of the presidential suite and a check up on the painting crew's progress."

Was it that time already? She glanced at the clock on her computer and shoved away from the desk with a gasp. "We're behind schedule! We were supposed to meet about it an hour ago. I am so sorry. I should've been at your office on time. I forgot." She rambled, as she rushed past him.

He caught her arm and tugged her back into him. "Lillian, slow down. I had a meeting that ran long. You're not in trouble, and there's no need to rush. The suite and the painters will still be there in a few minutes. No need to endanger yourself running through a construction site."

She settled, the blush returning. "I...I'm sorry."

He tucked a wayward curl behind her ear with a soft smile. "No need to apologize. I told you. You aren't in trouble. Now, let's walk to the elevator with a little less need for speed. Maybe I need to start calling you my little speed demon instead."

The blush turned to a fire in her ears and cheeks. "I'm not a speed demon!"

"You're right. Much too well-behaved for that. I guess we'll just have to stick with your established nickname, hmm? Little miss..."

She shivered and looked away. "Can we go?"

"Of course." He released her and offered an arm. "Shall we, milady?"

"What is wrong with you?" She laughed, but linked her arm through his. "We look silly, and people are going to stare."

He tugged on a strand of her wild hair where it had escaped her ponytail. "Do I look like I care?"

She pulled back, jerking her arm out of his. "You should."

He frowned. "I never have before, and I'm not about to start now. Come on. We should go check on the painting crew's progress and see how the suite looks now that it's fully decorated."

Sucking a deep breath to steady herself, she tugged her skirt down and hurried after him with a tight smile. She had to stop giving in to the temptation to go with the flow he established. If she didn't, she could endanger her professional image, not to mention her standing with her brother. She'd worked far too hard at work to have her team talking behind her back about gaining promotions by sleeping with the boss, and she didn't want Tyler angry at her either.

He took her by the elbow and guided her out of the room, giving her no chance or room to protest that someone might see. His stern look when she tried to adjust herself shut down any attempt at it very quickly. She remained silent the rest of the way to the presidential suite.

Once they reached the suite, she drifted through the room, looking at the decor. It was stately and simplistic, though she knew the paintings on the walls alone cost thousands of dollars. The rug under her feet was lush and an inviting shade of blue. The bed was piled with pillows and partially obscured by the canopy on one side. She drifted over, brushing her fingers over the cherry wood frame supporting the canopy.

Atticus stood in the doorway, hands in his pockets. "It looks lovely. Should we check the bathroom?"

She headed that way, stepping into a massive bathroom that boasted a whirlpool bath, a shower, and a steam room. The sinks were marbled granite with gleaming platinum fixtures, and a gilt gold mirror hung over them. The muted cream paint job brought everything together well. Turning back to the mirror, she found Atticus standing behind her, a slight smile on his lips.

"Everything to your liking?" she whispered.

He gave her an appraising look. "Maybe. I might need a closer look."

She turned to face him, heart thudding. He wasn't talking about the room anymore. Of that, she was certain. His gaze flicked to her lips and then back to her eyes. A shiver worked its way down her spine. If he just leaned in a little and pressed his lips to hers, it would turn into the same fantasies she'd dreamed about for years.

He stepped closer, reaching out to run his thumb over her cheek in slow circles. "A much closer look, I think," he whispered.

The shiver intensified into a wave of longing. Her gaze fell on his full mouth, and she wondered for the second time that day what it would be like to have his mouth on hers. He bent his head until their foreheads touched, and when his hands drifted to her hair, tangling there, she closed her eyes with a sigh. She shouldn't let him do this. She should stop him.

She didn't.

His mouth brushed hers in a maddeningly brief moment. She whimpered when the contact disappeared. Then she was rewarded with a real kiss, his lips caressing hers as he tugged on her hair to pull her head back so he could really kiss her. His mouth demanded her submission, and when he urged her to let him deepen the kiss, she opened to him with a sigh. He groaned, his hold on her tightening. His free hand gripped her hip and dragged her into him. She flushed when the close contact left her without doubts about his interest in her and their kiss.

When he finally pulled back, she sucked in a shuddering breath, goosebumps trailing down her arms. She stared up into his dark gray gaze and then back to his mouth and the attractive shadow of stubble gracing his jaw, fingers going to her lips. The shock gradually gave way to panic. What had she just done? She'd let Atticus Moore kiss her. She'd liked it every bit as much as she'd imagined she would.

She backed away, the small of her back pressing into the marble sink's counter. "That…"

"…was amazing," he murmured, his gaze returning to her mouth.

She flinched even though she desperately wished she could voice her own agreement. Instead, she forced herself to shake her head and disagree with him. "That can't happen again, Atticus."

"Why not? Didn't you like it?" He reached out to toy with a strand of her hair with his long, slender fingers.

"We can't. You're my boss, and Tyler—"

"…can screw off," Atticus said bluntly. "I love your brother like my own, but I'm not going to forgo pursuing what I want to please Tyler."

She shrank away from him. "My professional image…"

"I will not do anything to damage that, little miss." His tone and gaze softened. "I promise you your job won't be in jeopardy."

"But it already is," she whispered back. "T-this changes things."

"For the better, I think."

She brushed past him, nerves frayed. How could fate be so cruel as to give her what she'd wanted for years at precisely the moment when she could least afford to let herself have it? She wanted so badly to go back into his arms and let him soothe her fears with another of those sizzling kisses, but she couldn't. He was her boss, and there were too many obstacles. "I don't think so."

"You do. You're just afraid to admit it."

"This can't happen again, Atticus." She turned and fled the room, leaving him to himself. She wasn't sure if she was relieved or disappointed when he let her go without comment.

Chapter 4

Atticus found her in the pool in the early afternoon after work was over for the day. It had been a few days since their first kiss. That kiss was all he could think about for days, but he'd forced himself to give Lillian a little breathing room. Tonight, that room ended if she'd let him have his way. He was going to show her that as scary as it was, he could help her soar if she'd just let go and let him have control. She didn't need to worry about her professional image or Tyler, and he would take her somewhere where neither would intrude if he had any say.

Lillian lay floating in the water, her unruly hair wrapped in a thick braid around her head. She'd never liked lounging on the pool floats like many other women he'd known, claiming she preferred the feeling of the water cradling her. He smiled and tucked his hands into his pockets, watching for a long moment while she was unaware of his presence.

Finally, he decided to break the spell. "Lillian?"

She startled, splashing out of her relaxed pose and coming up to tread water, eyes wide. When she spotted him, she relaxed with a groan. "Really, Atticus...was that necessary?"

He shrugged. "How else would I get your attention?"

She swam in lazy strokes to the steps and climbed out, water streaming over her lithe frame. He watched her, shifting his weight from foot to foot a bit. The woman had no idea what she did to him or how infuriating it was to wait for her to towel off when he wanted nothing more than to seduce her here and now, showing her how flimsy all of her excuses were.

He restrained himself with a tiny growl. No. He was not a savage, and he could wait. He would wait until tonight after dinner. He'd timed this carefully to make certain they wouldn't be done in time to return after dinner. There would be no seduction until he'd taken her to dinner and eased her defenses with a reminder of how well they'd gotten along in the past before he'd become her boss. If he pushed now, she'd only rebuff him again and refuse to attend dinner.

"What did you need?" She unwound the braid from her hair and started toweling it dry as she approached.

He eyed the slippery floor and her quick steps, his protective instinct rising. "Slow down before you slip, little miss."

She slowed immediately, cheeks flushing. "I'm not a child."

"I think we've well established that." He crossed the distance between them and took the towel from her, helping her dry the water out of her hair.

"Thank you." Her tone was hushed and shy.

He smiled. She'd always liked it when he helped her with her hair after pool parties when they were kids, too. Now it had a much different tone than it had then, but he still enjoyed caring for her as much as she seemed to enjoy letting him do it. So few people took care of the little girl standing in front of him, she least of all.

Tyler had tried, but he'd been spread too thin acting as both breadwinner and single parent. Atticus was older than Tyler by three years, more settled by then, and able to be around to help his friend out after Tyler and Lillian had lost both parents in a car crash. Tyler had relied on Atticus to help when he couldn't. Back then, looking for the family his own had never been, he'd been only too happy to give someone else what he hadn't had, and he hadn't minded helping Tyler out. Tyler had been the brother he'd never had, after all. Now, even though Tyler hadn't asked him to take care of the young woman in front of him, and would probably kill him if he saw the shift in Atticus's motives for doing it, he still found himself wanting to make sure she was cared for and happy. Once in a while, it would do her good to let someone—preferably him—look after her.

"What did you come for?" she murmured, relaxing into his touch with a sigh.

"I'm taking my yacht out to the big island. Come with me."

"What for?"

"Dinner. Maybe to go see some of the other resorts and casinos I built there. You've been working very hard, Lillian. Let me do something nice to reward you."

She pulled away, turning to face him. "Just us?"

"Just us."

"Why isn't anyone else coming? They've worked hard too."

He took her by the hips and pulled her close, wrapping the towel around her shoulders as a shiver wracked her. She was dampening his suit, but for once, he didn't feel any urge to fuss about the damage or the mess. He could afford to replace it if the cleaner couldn't remove any water stains, and he liked how she trembled when the finely woven wool cloth of his suit jacket scraped along the bare skin of her belly and ribcage. After making her wait a moment for an answer, he finally said, "I want to spend some time with just you, that's why. Do you have plans?"

She rested her palms against his chest and resolutely stared down at her hands. "No."

"Then come with me."

Still, she hesitated.

"What are you afraid of, Lillian?"

Her chin lifted, her beautiful green eyes finally meeting his. A sheen of uncertainty veiled them.

He cupped her cheek in his palm with a frown. "Lillian? What is it? What's wrong?"

"It's not fair," she whispered. "It's not fair. Life dangling this in front of me when I can't have it."

He dipped his head to brush his nose against hers. "Lillian Miller, life isn't dangling anything in front of you. I'm right here, within easy reach. I'm not going anywhere, and you most certainly can have me, if you'll just let go and let me take charge."

She closed her eyes with a sigh. "I c-can't."

"Can't let go or can't let me take charge?"

"Neither." Her voice was raw. "I can't have you."

He kissed the tip of her nose. "Not true, little miss. Let me prove it to you. Go to dinner with me."

She lifted her gaze to his. "I want to…"

"Then you will." He scooped her up and headed outside the pool house into the muggy summer air.

She clung to him with a sigh. "It's not that easy."

"Oh, but it is." He grinned. "Let go, remember? I'll prove to you it's much easier than you think."

***

Lillian sat at the dinner table in his yacht's private dining room, watching in shock as a waiter settled a dish of perfectly cooked salmon in a lemon butter sauce in front of her. When Atticus had said he wanted to take her to dinner, she hadn't expected this. He'd parked the yacht on his private docking pier and brought the restaurant from one of his resorts to her. She stared at him from across the table, unable to quite form the words for the situation.

He smiled back as another waiter placed a steak in front of him. A dish of seasoned vegetables and a salad were placed between them at the center of the table. The two waiters poured them both full glasses of the same Ace of Spades brand she'd recommended using for the grand opening's champagne selection. This one was their Rosé.

She watched the waiters pour in numb silence. A bottle of this stuff costed at least three hundred dollars. It wasn't something you just popped open for a private two-person dinner like this. Not in her world, anyway.

When the waiters retreated, she took a tentative sip of the wine, savoring the sweet fruity flavor and the hints of smoky grilled notes behind it.

"Good?" Atticus asked, sipping his own as he watched her with his keen gray eyes.

She nodded, stomach rumbling. The salmon smelled wonderful too. The two of them ate in silence for a while until she finally worked up the courage to ask him what she'd been wanting to ask since the pool house. "Atticus?"

"Yes?"

"What did you mean when you said you'd show me how easy it is if I let go?"

He smiled at her with the affectionate look she'd only seen directed at her. It softened the angular planes of his face and the sharp look in his eyes. "I meant I'd show you it's easy to be with me. Physically, emotionally...in every way that counts. I know you have fears, Lil. I know you're unsure how we would balance things to avoid wrecking your career, and I know you're scared for other reasons that you won't share. This is real...we are real."

She picked at the rest of her salad. "How can I be sure? I'm risking so much if I say yes to this, Atticus. My relationship with my brother, my job, you..."

"First of all, you're not risking your job," he replied. "That will not be affected by anything between us no matter what happens. If you decide after tonight, you still don't want to move forward and can honestly say it's not just because you're afraid. Then I'll leave this be and will remain nothing but professional in private or otherwise. But if you can't..." His look turned from affectionate to ravenous. "Then I will have all of you, Lillian, whether or not you are afraid. In exchange, I promise you will have all of me and everything I can offer. But that can only happen if you're willing to take a risk tonight."

"What kind of risk?"

"Let me prove to you we have the chemistry to make this work, not just the comfortable camaraderie we had as children or the easy friendship we have when working together."

She blushed, shifting in her seat. Could she really do that? If she did, she'd be crossing a line she'd never crossed with her ex. In truth, she wasn't just afraid of this because she feared Tyler's reaction or endangering her career. She knew Atticus well enough to know he'd do nothing to hurt her professional image. Even if she didn't want to remain with the company, he'd find her something else and make sure she would be okay there.

This was something more.

It was about past wounds and her fears that if she trusted Atticus, it would do more than garner Tyler's ire or start rumors in the office. She feared it would break her in much worse ways than having the one man she'd trusted in college sleep with her college roommate and close friend because she wasn't ready to put out.

"What's going on in that head of yours, little miss?" Atticus asked softly.

"Atticus, if...I don't want it to hurt."

His brow furrowed in concern. "Don't want what to hurt, love?"

"When it falls apart...I...I just don't—"

He was up in an instant and crossing to her side. Kneeling, he took her hands in his. "Lillian, listen to me. I have no intention of going anywhere. If you want me, I'm going to take you. You know I never give up until I have what I want, and that's you this time."

"But what if it's not me tomorrow?" she whispered, heart aching.

"I don't work like that." He squeezed her hands. "You know I don't. If there's anything you should be afraid of, it should be that I will consume you until you don't know which way is up and which down. I never do things in half measures. Let me prove it to you in just a small way tonight."

She lowered her head to hide behind her hair, a tremble in her voice. "Atticus, I...I might mess up."

"Mess up?" He reached up to cup her cheek in his palm. "Little miss, there is no way you could do that tonight unless you demand I take you back to the island and refuse to try to trust me. Even if you do that, I will not be angry."

Her eyes remained permanently fixed on their intertwined hands. "You d-don't understand," she said. This was harder than she could have imagined. Her past fears were at the fore now, and there was no way she could suppress them. She had to deal with this. It was now or never.

He sighed and pulled her from her chair into his lap, cradling her to his chest. "I'm trying. Help me to, Lillian."

"I t-trusted someone else not to be angry with me f-for not knowing what to do, and h-he ditched me for my friend," she admitted.

"What?" His tone hardened.

"I wasn't ready, so he said h-he'd find someone who was." She curled into him, a deep sense of relief warring with shame at the confession.

"Oh, Lil," he whispered, his grip tightening. "That man was an idiot and a jerk. I promise you I'll never be angry at you for inexperience or for saying no if you're not ready. I will understand if you don't want to be with me like that tonight. I promise. If you do, I will consider it an honor."

She clung to him, the shame easing. "You really mean I can't do anything wrong?"

"I really do." He stood and picked her up, heading for the bedroom on the yacht. "If you want this, all you have to do to please me is let go and let me take charge. I'll take care of you, Lillian, just like always."

A tiny shiver skittered through her, and she wrapped her arms around his neck with a sigh, relaxing. She wanted this badly. She could have this, just as Atticus had said. He didn't mind her inexperience, and she didn't know anyone she trusted more than him to be her first. "You'll be gentle? I...it's my first time."

He sucked in a sharp breath, setting her down on the bed and staring down at her with an inscrutable expression. "Really?"

"Really…" She looked away, afraid to see his reaction.

The bed dipped, and he sat beside her, turning her face up to his and kissing her thoroughly. When she was breathless and melting against him, he released her mouth and said, "I'll be gentle, baby girl. You just have to trust me, and I'll make it as good as I can."

She nodded, sagging into him. "I trust you."

Chapter 5

Lillian woke in the warm cocoon of the sheets and comforter on Atticus's bed. She stretched, smiling at the slight soreness the movement provoked. They really had gone through with it last night. She'd given Atticus her virginity, and in the warm light of the morning sunshine streaming in through the window, she felt like she was floating on cloud nine.

Atticus had already risen, but his side of the bed was warm, so he'd only been up for a few minutes at most. She heard murmurs of conversation from the office connected to the yacht's master bedroom. Sitting up, she located the dress she'd worn last night and pulled it on, wishing she'd brought a change of clothes to go home with. Creeping to the door, she raised a hand to knock when she heard Tyler's voice in the small office. Peering in, she saw Atticus was focused on his laptop. Tyler must have called.

"...not going to just stand aside while you screw around with my sister. You're nearly ten years older than she is! What are you thinking? Or are you thinking at all? You'll ruin her! She's practically your sister."

Atticus cleared his throat, silencing even Tyler's tirade with a thunderous look. "Tyler Miller, your sister is a grown woman, not a little girl. She is not my sister, however close we all were growing up, and what I feel for her is certainly not brotherly affection. I am not screwing around with her, as you so rudely put it, and she didn't seem concerned with the age gap, so I don't think you need to concern yourself either. You are my best friend, but that woman out there is my heart and soul." Atticus's voice sharpened. "I will not lose her in order to make you feel more comfortable. I only called because I thought it right to inform you before you find out some other way."

"I can't believe you!" Tyler's voice rose in disbelief and anger.

"Believe it. You know how much I care about your sister, Ty. I always have. I'd never do anything to intentionally hurt her—"

"You keep up with this, and that's exactly what you'll do! What do you think will happen when you tire of her and leave?"

"Tyler Miller!" Atticus's tone sharpened. "Suggest that again, and we'll come to blows when I next see you. Your sister isn't a fling, and you know full well I take relationships seriously."

"I don't give my approval. Doesn't that matter to you at all, Atti?" Tyler's tone was almost pleading now. "She's my baby sister."

"The only thing you have right about that, Tyler, is that she is your sister. But she hasn't been a child in a very long time. Your problem is that you can't see it. I do."

"You know what, Atticus?" Tyler's voice tightened. "If you won't quit playing games with my sister, I don't want to hear from you again, and you can bet Lillian will be hearing from me."

Atticus growled, low and menacing. "I'm not playing any games with Lil. You'll be waiting a very long time to hear from me again if this is how you're going to behave!" The laptop screen slammed down with startling force.

Lillian backed away from the door, chest tightening. What had she done? She'd done precisely what she'd been trying to avoid—coming between two best friends and angering her brother. She never should have given in to Atticus, vulnerable and needy or not. She'd wanted him so badly last night and let him have her without protest. She should have known better.

She fled to the bathroom, turning on the shower to hide her heavy breaths. Now, even though it killed her even to consider it, she had to walk away from Atticus. She couldn't get between them, and she couldn't risk her career for it either. Atticus would understand, wouldn't he?

His words to Tyler came back then. That woman out there is my heart and soul. How had she not noticed Atticus Moore was in love with her? She'd known him nearly all her life, and she knew he wouldn't lie to Tyler, even if he wouldn't say the words aloud. She stood under the hot water, body shaking. It figured that the one man who really loved her for who she was happened to be the one man she couldn't let herself have or want.

She swiped at her eyes filled with tears threatening to fall, and got out of the shower. No sense in prolonging this. She needed to steel herself for this, and find a way to lie to Atticus about how she felt about last night. It hurt so badly to consider lying to a man she knew trusted her to be honest, and was banking on her honesty to pull them through the initial hurdles toward a future. Now she had to crush it to keep their relationship from ruining one he'd always held in high regard. She wouldn't get between Tyler and Atticus. There were other men to love.

She knew it wasn't true even as she thought it. There might be other men to love, but there were no other men she would ever love. She'd tried with her ex, and her fixation on Atticus had been the subconscious block that kept her from sleeping with her ex, ultimately leading to his devastating betrayal. Trying again wouldn't see better success now, not after she'd let Atticus have her body as well as her soul.

Pinching some color into her cheeks, she took a few steadying breaths. It didn't matter that this would rip her heart out and break his for a time. She had to do this for his sake. If she really loved him, she couldn't be why he lost the few genuine and close relationships he had in his life.

***

When Lillian came out of his bathroom, he knew something was wrong with one look on her face. He was still seething over the call with Tyler. The man could be so bull-headed sometimes, and this was an occasion where he'd decided to be just that. He hated that the call had to end on such bad footing, but he wasn't budging on this. Lillian was his. Tyler would have to deal.

Seeing Lillian's distant expression, which didn't quite hide the regret and pain in her eyes, wiped away all concern over Tyler. He froze, unsure what could have happened between last night and this morning. "Lil?"

She looked away. "I want to go back."

"We don't have to hurry back. I told the team we'd be out until late this afternoon."

Her jaw tightened, as she continued avoiding his gaze. "I want to go back, Atticus. Now."

"Are you okay?"

"No. Last night..." Her voice wavered. "Last night was a mistake. I...I felt vulnerable, and it sounded so...I shouldn't have given in."

A low growl built deep inside of him. She was doing it again. Refusing herself things she wanted and had no reason to push aside because she thought she shouldn't. "This had better not be like turning down the last piece of cake on your birthday, little miss."

"Don't call me that," she hissed. "You're nothing more than my boss, and it needs to stay that way."

"No, it most certainly does not, and you weren't saying that last night in my bed." He shoved his hands into his pockets to hide the way they were shaking. Why was she doing this? "You promised me not to run from this if last night went well. You're many things, sweetheart, but a good actress isn't one of them."

"I don't want more between us," she insisted.

"You do. You just don't want to risk everything else to have it." He stalked closer, grabbing her chin and forcing her to look at him. "What did I tell you, Lillian? First rule of engagement. What is it?"

"No lies," she whispered, meeting his gaze.

"Are you lying to me?"

"No."

"I don't believe you. Tell me the truth."

She sucked in a sharp breath, color rising into her cheeks from how close they were. Flashes of last night came back to her, unrelenting.

No! she thought as she shoved him away. "How dare you accuse me of lying on purpose? This isn't a game, Atticus."

"No, it most certainly is not." He gritted his teeth. "I know you enjoyed last night. Tell me the truth. Why are you pushing me away?"

Her hands trembled at her sides. "Stop, Atticus. Please…"

The word, soft and broken, stabbed him to the quick. What was wrong? Had he done something to cause her pain and her anger? "Come on, little miss," he whispered in a plea of his own. "Talk to me."

She shook her head and turned her back, wrapping her arms around her torso. "Take me home, Atticus."

He sighed. "Lil…"

"No. I mean it. Take me home right now. This...whatever this is…is a mistake. I don't want to talk about it. I don't even want to think about it. I want to go back—"

"We can't," Atticus said, voice strangled.

"Maybe we can't," she agreed before delivering the final blow. "But I can. I want to go back to the hotel and work, sir."

Shoulders slumping, he slipped past her. "Very well."

Chapter 6

Atticus made it through a week of burying himself in work and avoiding Lillian before he had to ask her questions that texts or phone calls couldn't answer. He was about to knock when her phone rang inside the office, insistent and demanding her attention. The ringing stopped. She must have picked up.

"Tyler, what's up?"

"Lillian." Tyler's voice was clipped and irritated on speaker. "I think you know why I'm calling."

"I'm not sure…"

"Don't play coy," he snapped. "What is the matter with you? He's ten years your senior, and he's your boss. Besides, he is like an older brother. How could you possibly—"

"Tyler, first of all, it's none of your business who I do and do not get involved with."

Atticus's hopes rose. Maybe last week had all been a misunderstanding. Maybe she'd panicked and said the first things that came to mind in order to get some space. If that was the case, she'd have to learn that asking would get further with him than anything else.

Her next words dashed his hope. "But if you must know, we're not an item. I made a mistake last week, and we slept together. That is not the same as being together, and you can rest easy knowing I've come to my senses," she snapped. "So, please...don't call to rub my face in my own rash behavior."

Tyler heaved a sigh over the phone. "You know this will complicate things for you. If you end up needing a job, my firm—"

"Atticus is mature enough not to let what happened impact my job. He'll get over it."

"He didn't seem inclined to get over it when he called last week. He seemed to believe you were the one."

Lillian remained quiet for a long moment.

"Lillian? You made sure he knew you weren't interested in more beforehand, didn't you?"

"Of course I did."

Atticus held back a growl. She'd done no such thing. In fact, she'd agreed to trust him, had promised to give them a chance if he could prove to her it was worth the risk. He'd thought he'd done so, but now he wasn't so certain. Maybe he'd made a huge mistake.

He left and headed back to his office, not wanting to hear more. She'd lied to her brother. Had she also lied when she'd told him on the yacht that she didn't want more between them? She seemed to be insistent on keeping her distance.

They hadn't talked at all on the ride home, and in the past week, she'd barely spoken to him if she could avoid it. When they saw one another in meetings, she was coldly professional, and when they ran across one another in the hotel, she quickly headed the other way to avoid him.

It cut deep. He couldn't think of a time they had been this uncomfortable around one another. And every time he saw her, he spotted the signs of exhaustion and misery in her.

He longed to reach out to brush her wayward curls out of her way in meetings or pull her aside to demand she take a day off to sleep long enough to remove the dark smudges of weariness beneath her eyes.

He resisted the urge even though it killed him to do it. She'd made herself clear, and any other attempts at conversation since the morning on his yacht had ended in disaster.

Anger and pain warred with one another inside, and he slammed his office door, stalking to his computer to turn on

39

his out-of-office email notification. The team didn't need him for the rest of the afternoon. He was going back to his mansion. He'd work out in his home gym and then take a dip in the pool to cool off some of his anger. Maybe some physical pain could take the edge off this emotional pain.

Never in his life had he experienced such pain. He'd gone through countless injuries in his younger years thanks to his reckless nature, but not one of them had ever hurt this badly. He wanted to scream and beat something to a pulp. Maybe Tyler.

He was almost certain she'd overheard his conversation with her brother. Even if she hadn't made up her mind before that to put distance between them, no doubt that conversation solidified it. And now that she'd lied to her brother, it would only be a matter of time before she chose to end things formally before they even started.

If he wanted any chance to salvage whatever small spark was left between them, he needed to blow off some steam and then confront her about avoiding him.

At the very least, he needed to be certain she was really being honest about how she felt about him if Tyler and her concerns about work were removed. If she hadn't lied to Tyler about her concerns over her job, then he knew at least that concern was not at the heart of the issue.

But hearing her lie to her brother so smoothly left him uncertain of even that much. If she could lie to him so easily, who knew what she'd told the truth or chosen to lie about?

For his own sanity, though, he needed to deal with this. He didn't run from his problems, and while Lillian had a habit of it, he was done putting up with that particular habit. She'd have to tell him face to face that she wanted to end the relationship.

He felt a pang deep in his chest at the thought of things ending. He'd respect Lillian's wishes if she truly thought they were a mistake, but he hated the idea with every fiber of his being.

Somehow, he'd already come to think of her as his, and what had happened that night on his boat only crystallized that for him. If she didn't think the same way, then for the first time in his life, he might actually find an obstacle he couldn't surmount. He might actually find himself heartbroken, not just disappointed, too, and the thought terrified him.

Chapter 7

A knock at her bedroom door pulled her out of the book she'd snagged from Atticus's library. Sighing, she threw her legs over the bed and stood, shuffling to the door to open it.

Atticus's butler, Graves, stood on the other side, hand poised to knock again. He lowered his arm with a smile when he saw her. "Miss Miller, Mr. Moore has requested your presence in his office."

She frowned. "What for?"

"He wishes to go over something about the hotel with you over dinner, unless you've eaten already."

Her stomach grumbled, reminding her that she hadn't eaten anything since lunch. She'd been too engrossed in her work and then too tired right after work to bother. "Just to go over the designs, right?"

"I believe so, Miss Miller. Shall I tell him you'll be up after you change?"

She glanced down at her yoga pants and t-shirt. Maybe she should change. Atticus was probably accustomed to wearing more formal attire to dinner, given his status, but she wasn't. He could deal with it. She wasn't trying to impress him. Besides, she sort of wanted to see his response. Would he be shocked? Off kilter? Or amused? "No. I'll go as I am. I can find my own way, Graves. Thank you."

He bowed and left, disappearing down the hall to return to his tasks. She sighed and returned to her room, putting a bookmark in the book she'd been reading. Then she pulled her hair into a high ponytail and trudged out of the bedroom to go see what Atticus needed this late. It was well after work hours, but it shouldn't surprise her. He spent most of his time working anyway, and he'd been worse than usual since their argument on the yacht.

She padded barefoot down the thick wine-red carpet that blanketed the oak floorboards of the mansion. Trailing her fingers along the banister, she looked down at the chandelier of the entryway and shook her head. He really did have a lot of money. She couldn't imagine owning a house with one chandelier, let alone one that had four like Atticus's mansion here did.

When she reached the heavy oak door of Atticus's office, she paused, collecting herself for a moment. She could still turn around and leave, and part of her wanted to. Still, he'd called her here to discuss their project. It would be childish and unprofessional not to appear when her boss called her. She might've ignored dress protocols because it was after hours, and they had known each other for so long, but she shouldn't refuse to show. Raising a hand, she knocked.

"Come in," Atticus called.

She opened the door and stepped inside.

He had two plates of chicken marsala and two glasses of chardonnay already resting on the desk, with the rest of the wine in a bucket of ice. A candle sat lit in the center, giving the whole scene a warm glow when paired with the dull orange light of the lamps around the room.

She didn't see any papers or his laptop, and she frowned. "Wasn't this supposed to be a business dinner?"

He stared back at her. "I had something I wanted to speak to you about, but you've been difficult to catch of late."

Flushing, she trailed over to the desk and sat across from him. "This looks romantic, not professional."

"Trust me. It's nothing of the kind," he muttered, voice sharpening. "I wanted you here to ask you a very blunt question, and I want the truth, Lillian."

Her heart hammered in her chest. "What are you talking about?"

"Us. You've been distant since the yacht, and I don't think it's because our night together wasn't good for you." He frowned at her. "I think you lied to me because you were spooked and overthought the situation, and I want the truth now. If you really want us to be over, I want you to look me in the eye and tell me that."

"I told you that on the yacht," she snapped, feeling ambushed.

"You were nearly in tears as you did so, which leads me to believe you didn't really want to say the words. If you can tell me that you want to end what's between us right now without looking near tears, I will let it go." He sipped at his wine, regarding her over the rim of his wineglass.

"I can," she whispered, heart aching. "As I said, we can't do this." She waved at the candle and the meal on his desk. "Any of this. I have a professional image to maintain, and—"

"Bull," he snapped, setting aside the wine. "You're using that as an excuse. You know full well I'd never let anything that happened between us hurt your career or your authority with those you're managing."

"People talk." Her voice rose in frustration. Why couldn't he understand this? Even if she knew he wouldn't intentionally jeopardize anything, he shouldn't dismiss her fears. "This is a hard limit for me, Atticus. I won't have my employees or coworkers claiming I got my position or upcoming promotion because I slept with my boss!"

"No one would say that. Everyone knows how hard you work. They respect you, and more importantly, they like you. Not one of them would dare imply that."

"They might not dare do so openly, but there'll be muffled gossip around the water cooler. They'll be thinking about it if they don't say it. It's just a bad idea!"

"Others have made it work. This isn't the problem at all, Lillian. Something else is at the root of this obstinance." He leaned back in his chair and crossed his arms, candlelight throwing his high cheekbones into sharp relief. "What's the real reason you don't want to be with me?"

She stood, throwing her hands up in exasperation. "You know what, Atticus? This is enough of a reason! You don't need an explanation at all, actually. I'm giving one out of respect for our friendship, but I didn't have to. You need to hear me spell it out? I don't want you. I don't want a relationship. I want to remain nothing more than an employee. Is that clear enough?"

A muscle in his jaw ticked as he stared back at her, but after a long moment, he looked away with a curt nod. "Fine. Get out."

"Really?" She shook her head with a huff. "Look, we still have to work together. We need to figure out how to do that despite—"

Atticus stood, towering behind his desk. "Lillian, leave. I'm not asking. You don't want to be anything more, and I will respect that, but I don't want to talk about it further, and I definitely do not want to eat a meal while pretending nothing is wrong. Take your food and the wine with you, and just go."

She contemplated the tired slump of his shoulders and the pain in his expression. He was hiding it better than she'd hid hers the morning after he'd taken her virginity, but it was there. Her choice was breaking his heart, something she hadn't really expected of Atticus. He was usually so composed and cool. It ached to watch him hurt, but this was for the best. She nodded, collected both the plate and the wine glass, and left him alone.

Chapter 8

The month remaining before opening slipped away at an agonizingly slow pace. Lillian couldn't shake the ache that had settled into her chest since she'd told Atticus they wouldn't see each other anymore. Tyler had called a few more times, but she'd barely spoken to him at all. Now the grand opening night was upon them.

She glided through the ballroom where they'd set up refreshments and over to the adjoining room of poker and roulette tables by a gleaming bar. Everything seemed to be in order, and the guests would arrive in a few minutes. Atticus would kick the evening off with the ribbon cutting to symbolize the hotel's opening, and then they'd have refreshments and a bit of friendly gaming near the bar.

Her phone rang in the pocket of her slacks, and she pulled it out. Tyler. Sighing, she flicked it to send it to voicemail. A minute later, the phone rang again. She rolled her eyes and picked up. "Tyler, I'm busy."

"You're always busy," he remarked. "I wanted to check in on you. You've been clipped and quiet every time you've picked up, and over the last month, you've ignored half of those calls entirely."

"Because I'm—"

"Busy?" Tyler finished.

"Yes. Much like now. I don't want to talk, Tyler. You've done enough."

"What?" He sounded confused.

She pinched the bridge of her nose and sighed. "I didn't...never mind. I'm just a bit tired and stressed. The grand opening will start seating for the opening ceremony in three minutes, and I need to be on stage in twenty. What do you really want, Tyler?"

"Initially, I just wanted to know things were really okay with you. Now I want to know what you mean by 'you've done enough'. What's going on?"

"You know what, Tyler? If you don't know, I don't want to share."

"I don't understand, Lil. What did I do?"

"Tyler," she snapped. "I don't have time to deal with this or with you. Really, I'm in no mood. I have to go on stage in twenty minutes with Atticus, and the guests are starting to arrive. I don't want to...It's going to be a long enough night without adding this to the list of things I have to find a way to slog through. Got it?"

"This is about Atticus, isn't it?" he asked quietly. "That's what you mean when you say I've done enough. You overheard us talking. I'm the reason you broke things off with him, aren't I?"

She swallowed hard and collapsed onto a bar stool as guests started trickling into the next room. Her feet already hurt thanks to these stupid heels, and Tyler was dredging up even more emotional pain. Even though she knew he deserved more grace because of all he'd done to raise her and care for her through the years after their parents' deaths, she couldn't muster the energy to be forgiving. "What does it matter, Ty? You got what you wanted."

"I—"

"Tyler, I really do have to go," she murmured.

"Sis, maybe—"

"Bye, Tyler. We'll talk some other time, but not if you decide to bring this up again. I'm not talking about it with you." She hung up, tucking her phone into her pocket. It buzzed again. Tyler was probably calling back, but she didn't have the energy for this.

It hurt badly enough to be forced to stand on the stage, smiling beside Atticus, when the mere sight of him sent pain slicing through her chest. She knew they didn't look happy when they were around each other anymore. They never really looked content or happy like they had before. Despite Atticus's promises, their quickly ended romance was already impacting both of their images. She just hoped she could put on a good show tonight so it wouldn't be obvious to the high-paying clients here.

***

Atticus stood still while Graves adjusted his tie and then disappeared to go help with the refreshments. He was grateful to his old friend and butler for being here to support him. He would've liked to have Tyler here instead, but his best friend was otherwise occupied, and after the way Tyler had come between him and Lillian, Atticus found himself disinclined to see the man.

His phone buzzed in his pocket, and he pulled it out to check the caller ID. Tyler. He rolled his eyes and picked up. If this wasn't an apology, he'd hang up as soon as he could get a word in. Now was not the time to deal with an argument. Lillian would be in any minute. As soon as he picked up, the other man lit into him.

"Why didn't you pick up earlier?"

An argument, then. He sighed. "I was busy. I'm sure you are aware we had the grand opening tonight."

"Yes, but...I need to ask you about Lillian. She's been avoiding my calls or answering them, but keeping everything brief and terse. It's not like her," Tyler said. "I'm worried."

Atticus ground his teeth for a moment before he replied. "You should be, Tyler."

"Excuse me? You sound like you think this is my fault!"

"You think it isn't, you idiot? If she hasn't told you so, it's only because she can't bear to upset you." His temper rose with his voice. "You knew very well that Lil would give up anything to make you happy, Tyler Miller! She loves you. More than that, she looks up to you and feels indebted to you because you raised her so she wouldn't end up in foster care after your parents died."

"Come on, Atti, it's not—"

"I'm not done, Tyler. The only thing she cares about more than her job is you, and you barged into our business, making her feel like she had to give up a chance to be happy with me to make you happy. I don't want to hear it from you." He blew out a heavy breath, softening his tone a fraction. "Tyler, she's miserable. She has dark circles under her eyes like she's not sleeping. I'm pretty sure she's lost weight. She looks worse than death warmed over. Don't you dare tell me this isn't your fault. She overheard you chewing me out for sleeping with her and intending to make her mine. I'm certain of it now, and she lied to you that day on the phone, by the way. She didn't tell me it was a fling."

Tyler remained silent, as though he didn't know what to say.

"Did you actively talk her into breaking things off, Ty?"

"No...I mean, not in as many words. It took me a week to cool off enough to talk to her, and when I did, I just asked her to confirm or deny it. I didn't talk her into it."

"But you planned to?"

The other side of the line went quiet. Finally, Tyler heaved a sigh. "Yes."

"She's miserable, Tyler. I hope you understand what you've done."

"Look, Atticus," Tyler snapped. "I get that you think I've done the wrong thing. She's probably not nearly as miserable as you think, and she'll get over it if she is. She's better off leaving early on before she gets hurt."

Atticus's fingers went stiff, and he barely got the words out when he replied. "That's not fair to me, and you know it. I'm not the sort of man who would take a relationship with her

49

lightly."

"I know my sister," he stated. "And I know you. It'll end with her getting hurt. This is for the best."

"You know what?" Atticus snapped. "You don't know what's best for her, Tyler. Not anymore. You know full well I never would've done anything to hurt her, and you know once I make up my mind, it's made up. She is the only one who would've walked away, and she did because of you, not because it was best for her."

"She decided herself."

"You know what, Miller? Don't call me again, or I'll block your number. You can call Lillian to apologize. We won't be speaking again if you don't intend to apologize to her. You don't have to worry about my relationship with her screwing up our friendship. You've done that yourself. We're through unless you fix your giant screw-up, understood?"

"Come on. Be—"

Atticus hung up with a growl. He clenched his fingers around his phone, tempted to hurl it at a wall. That wouldn't do much. It was Tyler's face he wanted to smash. His phone didn't need to withstand his wrath. After what he'd just heard from Tyler, he was certain he'd screwed up too by letting Lillian go. This was done. He was through waiting for this.

After that call, he needed time to steel himself before seeing Lillian and knowing he would forever feel that sharp blast of pain, longing, and regret that blew through his walls every time he saw her. There wasn't any time left, though. The low buzz of the crowd's chatter filled the space, and he glanced at the clock on the wall above the stage entrance. It was time.

Where was Lillian?

His frustration rose.

He could understand her need to push him away because of Tyler, but she should've just said that. He probably would've taken his anger out on Tyler and forced him to stop being such a moron about the issue, but he would've understood. Instead, she'd lied, which made him almost as furious with her as he was with Tyler.

The door to the casino opened, and she appeared, dressed in a pair of fitted slacks and a ruffled white blouse that dipped just low enough to expose a tantalizing glimpse of her cleavage. He stared for too long, wishing he could remind her of how good things were between them, so she'd stop pushing him away. But he'd promised to respect her decision, so he dragged his gaze back up. "It's time. You're late."

"Sorry," she whispered.

He dared a glance at her face and found nothing, but his own misery reflected on him. Nothing about her tense shoulders, the tight set of her jaw, or the weak attempt at a smile she offered spoke of a woman happy with her life. He'd never seen her look so lackluster as she did tonight. His anger softened a bit when he realized her lies had hurt her even more than they'd hurt him. She'd dished out her own punishment for the dishonesty. They still needed to talk, but he needed to tread gently with her to avoid making this worse.

"Let's go." He offered Lillian an arm. "Smile for me?" he whispered. "Just for tonight? I...you look miserable, little miss."

She looked away, but not before he saw the sheen of tears in her eyes. "Don't call me that, Atticus. I can't...I don't like it."

"Just one smile, Lil. Just while we're on stage," he begged.

"If you can manage one, then so will I."

He nodded, wishing that wasn't such a difficult thing to accomplish. Taking a deep breath, he shoved the pain back into its safe deep inside his heart and plastered a smile on his face. He'd put on a smile for her for tonight, but they would deal with this little issue and her lies when this was over. With a deep breath, he led Lillian into the dazzling lights.

Chapter 9

Lillian hid in the library, trying to avoid everyone, especially Atticus. The rest of the crew would be going back to the States tomorrow. She was supposed to stay on to help Atticus begin some other design work for a set of rental condos he wanted to construct near the hotel to provide more permanent vacation housing on that side of his island. It would be a month of torture being so close to him with no one else to take his attention off her.

A throat clearing caused her to jump to her feet, dropping the book she'd been pretending to read with a thump on the blue carpet. She stared up into familiar gray eyes, heart thudding in her chest. Words failed to come to mind as she tried to think of something to say. He looked ready to explode with anger, and she wasn't sure if it was directed at her or something else. She dropped her gaze, fiddling with her blouse's buttons.

"We need to talk. You'd best answer the questions I'm about to ask honestly this time, because I'm really not in the mood for lies."

She gasped, lifting her gaze to his with heat rising in her cheeks. "What?"

"You heard me. I believe I've made it clear how I feel about lies." His expression softened a little. "The truth, if you please."

"I…" She shifted from foot to foot, nervous about where this was going. "I don't know why you think I've been lying."

"I asked you if you really wanted to end our relationship in my office last month," he said quietly.

Oh. That was what this was about. She stared down at the floor without a word.

"I already know you lied to me. You didn't want to end anything. You did it because you knew Tyler didn't want us together, and you were afraid to wreck his relationship with me or to lose him yourself."

There was nothing left to say. He was right, and shame filled her. She should've been honest about why she wanted to end things, but instead, she'd run. In truth, she hadn't wanted to end it at all. That one night with Atticus had replayed in her dreams countless times since, leaving her sleepless many nights. She was miserable without him now that she'd tasted the fantasy she'd held since she was a teenager.

"I'm sorry." Her voice hitched, and then the stress and pain from the last month came to a head, as she collapsed into the leather armchair. "I'm sorry."

He sighed, motionless for a long moment.

She squeezed her eyes shut and buried her face in her hands. He probably hated her now. She'd known how he felt about lies and had lied anyway, not once, but twice. Firm, gentle hands picked her up and dragged her into a warm embrace. Then she was nestled on Atticus's lap as he sat down in the chair with her. "Thank you for being honest with me. Now this time, I want the truth, Lil. Do you or do you not want to take a chance on us?"

She buried her face in his chest. "If you still want m-me after this."

He stroked her hair gently. "Of course I do. I never stopped wanting you, but from now on, you will tell me the truth when something's wrong instead of running. We will find our balance, baby girl, even if it takes time. You just have to work with me. Promise me?"

"I promise."

"Good. Now, we're making a weekend trip to go see Tyler.

You're going to tell him yourself that we're together, and he can screw off if he doesn't like it."

"What?" She sat up. "But he'll—"

He scowled, a touch of his earlier anger back in his angular features. "If he knows what's good for him, he'll apologize. I've already informed him that if you don't get an apology, I'm through speaking to him."

She stiffened. "But Atticus, he's your best friend?"

"No one comes before the woman I love, little miss." He smiled at her affectionately. "Not even your brother."

***

They arrived at Tyler's small condo back in New York City in the early evening hours after an eight-hour flight on Atticus's private jet. Atticus propelled her up the steps and reached out to ring the bell when her hands were shaking too much to do so. She hated conflict with Tyler, and this news was certain to cause just that.

Tyler opened the door with a frown, eyes widening when he saw the two of them on his doorstep. She looked back at Atticus, who was standing there with his hands in his pockets and a stern look on his face. Then she looked back at Tyler and played with the strap of her purse. "T-Tyler…"

"Lil." He scowled at Atticus. "What are you both doing here?"

"Visiting to share some wonderful news," Atticus said, resting a hand on the small of her back. "Lil?"

Tyler groaned. "Oh, God, please no...Lil, don't tell me you're...didn't you...well, you know?"

She flushed. "Tyler Miller! I am not sharing those kinds of things with you."

"Well, someone's got to ask," he snapped. "Mom and Dad would have, but they're gone, so now I have to. If you mess up and get knocked up, I'm the one you'll be coming to."

Her temper washed away any trepidation she'd felt. "After

how you handled the news of my involvement with Atticus? You've got to be delusional! I'd go to Atticus before I'd go to you, whether he and I were involved. But I'm not here because he knocked me up. I'm here to tell you I've done some thinking and want to pursue a relationship with Atticus. Nothing you can say can talk me out of it. I let you do that once, and I was so miserable I didn't think I could keep going through it for another day."

Tyler scowled and crossed his arms. "Did you put her up to this, Atticus?"

Lillian didn't give Atticus a chance to answer. "No, he did not. Get your head out of the sand, Tyler. Stop allowing your protectiveness of me and your prejudice against Atticus because of his age and your discomfort with your best friend dating your sister to turn you into a jerk. It's not becoming. I'm standing here telling you I have decided to be with Atticus. I decided, not him. You either live with it or don't. It won't change what I do."

Lillian huffed out, drawing closer to Atticus. Seconds later, her eyes softened. "This man was there for me in every way he could be when we were dealing with Mom and Dad's deaths. He helped you when you couldn't cope with everything, and even though he now sees me as a woman instead of a child— something you ought to try—he still stands up for me and does his best to care for me. I love you, but I won't walk away from a man who loves me like that just to make you happy."

Tyler stood there in stunned silence for a few moments, staring at her as if she'd grown two heads. Finally, he cleared his throat and nodded. "Okay. Okay, I get it. I...I don't like it, but you're right. This isn't my decision. I'm sorry I tried to get involved, Lillian. Atticus...You hurt her, and I will rip you to pieces, best friend or not. Got it?"

Atticus laughed. "Got it. You going to leave us on the doorstep all day?"

Tyler sighed and glanced at Atticus's Maserati. "No. Bring the car into the garage. Can't believe you brought such an expensive car into this neighborhood. Hurry up and get it out of sight before someone gets ideas."

Atticus took her hand in his and drew her into him, kissing her temple. "Go inside and talk with your brother, little miss. I'll be in after I park the car."

She nodded with a soft smile.

When he was out of earshot, Tyler eyed her. "You really love him, don't you?"

"I do."

He nodded. "I'm sorry, Lil. Really...I should've known better. Should've trusted your judgment."

"Yes, you should've." She linked her arm through his and tugged him inside. "But I won't hold it over your head forever. Now come on. We have catching up to do."

Epilogue

A year later

Lillian rolled out of her side of the king-sized bed in Atticus's New York City penthouse apartment with a moan, clapping a hand over her mouth.

Atticus stirred and sat up. "Are you all right, love? You're not coming down with something, right before the wedding, are you? This is the third day in a row you've woken up feeling queasy."

She shook her head, fighting down the rising wave of nausea. It wouldn't settle, and it intensified instead. She shot to her feet and ran for the bathroom, making it just in time to heave into the toilet. Nothing much besides bile came up, and she was thankful she hadn't tried to eat anything yet.

Atticus's fingers scraped her hair back and off her neck. He tied it off with a ponytail with a sigh. When the heaving subsided, he handed her a glass of water. She took it with a tired, grateful smile and took small sips to settle her stomach, staring at the glittering diamond on her ring to ground herself. It would soon be replaced with a much more expensive gold band of small diamonds surrounded by rubies, but she liked the small single diamond encased with delicate gold prongs and filigree.

"Maybe we should see the doctor. Do you think we'll have to postpone the wedding next week?"

She shook her head with a grimace. "No. It's in the afternoon. I'll be fine by then."

He raised a brow. "You can time the puking?"

A weak laugh escaped her. "No, I can't time the puking, Atticus. It's better in the afternoons."

"It is?" He eyed her dubiously. "That doesn't make sense. Either you're sick, or you're not."

"I'm not."

He gestured to the toilet with a shake of his head. "Then what does this classify as?"

"Morning sickness?"

He opened his mouth to say something and then stopped, eyes widening. "Wait...you mean..."

She smiled. "Pretty sure, yes. I took the test last night, but you came home too late for me to tell you."

"We're going to have a baby?" he whispered.

"Yeah." Her smile faltered. "You're...You're okay with that, right?"

"Okay with it?" He cupped her face in his hands and kissed her. "I'm more than okay with it."

She relaxed against him with a contented sigh. "Oh, good. We hadn't talked about it, so I was worried...I mean, you seemed less than thrilled, so..."

"I'm just surprised. I didn't expect it quite so soon. We weren't trying, and you were on birth control, so I thought you wouldn't..."

"So did I, but I missed a dose by accident. Sometimes this stuff happens." She pressed her palms to her belly. "You're glad it did, though, right?"

"Yes, little miss." He kissed the tip of her nose. "Are you?"

"Well, I could do without the morning sickness." She laughed. "But yeah...yeah, I am. It took a few hours for it to really sink in after I had the test results staring back at me, but I'm more excited than I'd expected."

He grinned. "We're going to be parents."

"I'm just glad the wedding is in a week," she muttered. "Otherwise, I'm pretty sure Tyler would kill you for this."

He chuckled. "He could try."

"I'd rather he didn't. I'm not interested in losing you for a long, long time yet." She leaned up to kiss his cheek. "I rather like the idea of becoming Mrs. Atticus Moore in a week. If Tyler tries to screw it up, he'll be the one in fear for his life."

"Such a hellion when you set your mind to it," he murmured, drawing her into an embrace. "Don't worry, though. Tyler's already agreed to be my best man. I'm pretty sure he's not going to kill me."

She stared at the big steam room with longing and sighed. "Good. Atticus?"

"Hmmm?"

"We can't use the sauna anymore until the baby's born. I read that online last night." She groaned, pressing a hand to her lower back. "And I ache everywhere."

"Come on then, silly girl." He tugged on one of her unruly curls with a laugh. "I'll knead the knots out for you if you come back to bed."

With a satisfied smile, she let him draw her into the bedroom and back to bed. When he did as promised and began working the knots and kinks out of her back, she relaxed into the mattress with a contented moan. How she'd ever been lucky enough to have the man she'd wanted since her high school days, she didn't know, but she would forever be grateful that he'd chosen her. She couldn't imagine a life without him, and they would exchange the vows that would bind them for the rest of their lives in a week. She looked forward to that and to whatever riding off into the sunset would bring their way next.

~ THE END ~

If you enjoyed *CEO Billionaire Daddy*, take a look at a sneak peek of the next book in the series: *Lawyer Billionaire Daddy*.

Prologue

Sophia Anderson stepped into the stuffy meeting room with a spring in her step. This would be her first real case since passing the bar. Finally, she had achieved her childhood dream, and she was part of an incredible team, alongside junior partner, Maria Martinez, her idol. She had previously worked with Maria as a paralegal and admired the woman greatly. To be invited to work with her as an associate on this case was a dream come true.

Sophia took her place at the table with a smile, leaning over to greet Maria. The older woman smiled back and nodded to her. The door on the opposite side of the room opened, and she settled into her seat, trying not to squirm like an excited schoolgirl. She knew this wouldn't be nearly as exciting in a week or two, but she'd loved her work as a paralegal and expected to love this too.

Her gaze lifted to the people entering from the other side of the meeting room. This would be the other team, the people they would have to beat if they wanted to get their client acquitted. When Sophia saw a familiar tall frame with piercing brown eyes and neatly combed dirty blond hair, she tensed and tried to stifle a gasp. Her breath hitched, strangling in her throat.

His gaze fell on her, and she spotted the tightening of his jaw. It was probably imperceptible to anyone else, but she knew it well. He was surprised too. He was better at hiding it than she was, though, and he moved to the head of the table across from Maria without missing a step.

Maria leaned over with a tight smile. "Try not to be intimidated, Soph. His bark is worse than his bite."

Sophia forced a laugh. His bark was certainly *not* worse

than his bite. Elijah Clarkson was not a man to be trifled with and was a good lawyer. Well, spectacular, actually, given his quick rise to senior partner at his firm. Why hadn't she realized a high profile case like this might draw him in? She was so screwed. Seeing him now brought the old feelings she'd held for him into sharp focus once again, and she shifted in her seat, avoiding his gaze. "I'm sure it is."

"I'd know," Maria murmured. "I dated the hard-nosed pain in the—"

Elijah's gaze was firmly on Sophia, weighing her down in the chair until she wanted to sink into it and hide. Whatever Maria was telling her in quiet murmurs was lost in the gravity of that look, and she couldn't help looking back. This was so bad.

Back in the day, since she was 8 and him 16, she and Elijah could argue until kingdom come, and the few times he'd been by to visit since his graduation from high school had proven their debates hadn't changed much. She didn't fear that she wouldn't be able to counter his arguments before the jury and judge.

Now, at 24, she feared her professionalism would be wrecked, losing her place in this case because of their past. She had to keep a lid on her attraction to him, that had been growing since she turned 16, and avoid letting on about their personal connection.

Will Sophia succeed in keeping her distance from her childhood crush, Elijah? What happens if what she fears the most plays out live and on national TV?

Book 2 now available on Amazon!

Printed in Great Britain
by Amazon

15419504R00041